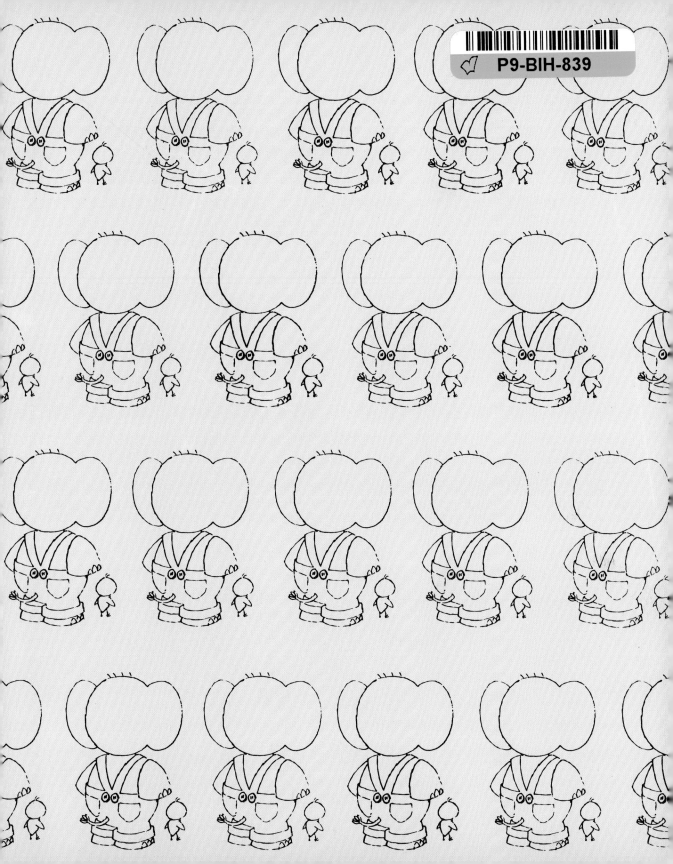

Bump's Umbrella

Christopher James

Illustrated by Steve Augarde

Baby's First Book Club

Bump the little elephant
was very proud. Bump had a
new umbrella that was two
different colors.

"It's lovely, Bump," said his
special friend, Birdie. "Now
when it rains, you will never
get wet."

Bump looked up at the clouds as they floated by.

"Is it going to rain, Birdie?" he asked.

"I don't think so," she said. "There are lots of fluffy white clouds, but only dark clouds bring the rain."

Although the sun was shining,
Bump still kept his umbrella open.
Soon, some of his other friends
came along.

He showed his new umbrella to
Little Bun and Big Bun. He showed
it to McDuff, the dog, and Munch,
the tortoise. Even the mouse stopped
his tricycle to say how nice it was.

Will
Bump fold
it up now?

"I have a shell, so I don't need an umbrella," said Munch.

But Bump was not listening.
He was looking at the sky. Bump
was hoping for just one dark cloud
to come along and make it rain.

"Don't step on Munch," called
Big Bun.

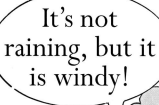

It's not
raining, but it
is windy!

By trying very hard not to step on Munch, Bump let go of his umbrella.

At that moment, the wind blew stronger and away it went.

"Come back!" he called, but the umbrella sailed on…

… and on, up into the sky.

When Birdie saw how upset
Bump was, she flew after the
umbrella. But the umbrella was
very big and Birdie was very small.
Rather than coming down again,
the umbrella carried Birdie
higher and higher.

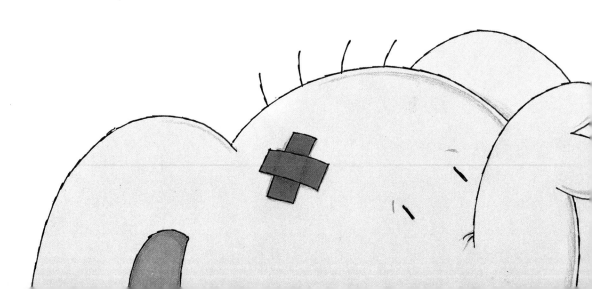

"Don't cry, Bump," said Little Bun. "Big Bun and I can run very fast. We'll soon find Birdie and your umbrella."

"Dogs are very clever at finding things," growled McDuff. "I'll find your umbrella in no time at all!"

The squirrels promised to search the treetops.

Which one will find the umbrella?

"Nobody can go as fast as me on my tricycle!" squeaked Whizzer Mouse, leading the way.

As for poor Munch, he wanted to help, but he was much too slow.

"It was all my fault," he sighed, curling up in his shell.

"You didn't mean it, Munch," said Bump.

Will they find Birdie as well?

Left all on his own, Bump felt very sad. Although he wanted his umbrella back, he wanted Birdie back even more.

To make things more miserable,
it suddenly became much darker.
"Oh, dear!" he said. "Now my
umbrella is lost and I think it is
going to rain."

Is it
a dark
cloud?

When Bump looked up in the
sky, it was not a dark cloud he saw.
Slowly floating down towards him
came his very own umbrella!
  But where was his special
friend Birdie?
  "Birdie! where are you?"
he called anxiously.

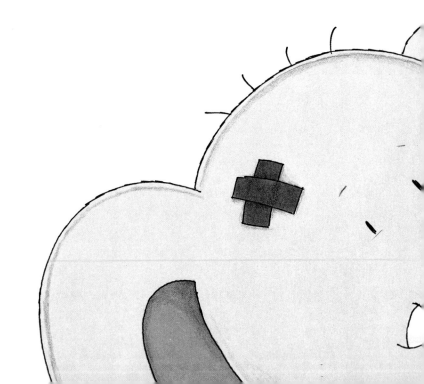

"I'm here!" whistled Birdie from the top of the umbrella. "My family saw your umbrella sail away and flew up to help me rescue it."

"You are clever!" cried Bump, reaching out to catch the handle. "It is nice to have my umbrella back again."

Look at Birdie and her familiy!

Then a dark cloud did arrive
to bring the rain. So Bump went
to find all the friends that had been
looking for his umbrella.

"Now it's your turn to help us."
Birdie told him. "Your umbrella is
big enough to keep us all dry."

"Except me," said Munch.
"I have my shell."

Did you enjoy Bump's story?